MW00891427

Sarah Martin Byrd

Debbie Wall

The manger mouse

by Sarah Martin Byrd

Illustrated by Debbie Wall

Ambassador International
GREENVILLE, SOUTH CAROLINA & BELFAST, NORTHERN IRELAND
www.ambassador-international.com

THE MANGER MOUSE

©2013 Sarah Martin Byrd

Illustrated by Debbie Wall

All rights reserved

Printed in the United States of America

ISBN: 978-1-62020-223-4
eISBN: 978-1-62020-321-7

Book layout & typesetting by Matthew Mulder
E-book conversion: Anna Riebe

AMBASSADOR INTERNATIONAL
Emerald House
427 Wade Hampton Blvd
Greenville, SC 29609, USA
www.ambassador-international.com

AMBASSADOR BOOKS
The Mount
2 Woodstock Link
Belfast, BT6 8DD, Northern Ireland, UK
www.ambassadormedia.co.uk

The colophon is a trademark of Ambassador

Manufactured by Color House Graphics, Inc.
Grand Rapids, MI, USA
Job# 40690

God has a perfect plan for even the meekest of His creations.

Matthew 11:29
Take my yoke upon you, and learn of me; for I am meek and lowly in heart: and ye shall find rest unto your souls.

It was very late on an unusually cold, damp, and frosty autumn night in that little town high up in the Judean Mountains. The early burst of winter had taken them all by surprise. Why, shepherds had not yet brought their sheep down from the hills!

All appeared quiet. Every living creature seemed to be sound asleep except Matty, the little brown stable mouse, and his mother.

Matty shivered, for this was the first time he had ever felt cold, and he was so tired his eyes felt like the wind had blown sand in them from the desert. All he wanted to do was fold into the warmth of his mother and sleep. But he couldn't, not until the Babe arrived.

"Mommy, is it time for the Babe to get here?"

"Shhhh, little one. You can rest assured we will see the miracle this night."

He wasn't sure what a miracle was, but he didn't want to miss it. Matty's mother told him he would be part of a holy happening. Matty didn't understand this either, for he was just a meek and lowly stable mouse.

But Matty trusted his mother. She would never tell a lie. Matty's mother told him he was to perform a great task tonight, a feat that no one but he would be able to do. Again Matty was confused by her words—but they made him feel very grown up and important.

Here in their cozy home burrowed into the mountainside, the other stable dwellers slept: Doris the Donkey, Molly the Cow, Tommy the Toad, Glenda the Goose, Randy the Rabbit, Lilly the Lamb, and Mrs. Margaret with all her chicks. But Precious the Moth was restless and fluttered ever so gently toward the opening of the cave where just a bit of light filtered in from the Innkeeper's lantern.

The sweet smell of hay mingled with the essence of the animals and their surroundings. The musky fragrance of moist earth hung in the air and mixed with the animals' strong scent. These odors are not pleasing to those unfamiliar with them, but Matty was used to the aroma and all the happenings in the stable, for he had never gone out of his home of clay.

But this night was different. It would someday become known as the first Christmas Eve.

It was also the chance for a wee stable mouse to be present at the birth of the Savior. Little did Matty know that he would be remembered for all time. God would use him in a mighty way, for he was to take part in the most important event in all of history.

Matty and his mother were not sleeping like the rest because they were preparing to accomplish a most important mission.

"It's busy time," said Matty's mother. "Follow me."

Late into the night Matty worked alongside his mother. As the whole world slept, they carried bits and pieces of straw to the feeding trough.

"This is the place where the mother of the King of Kings will lay him," said Matty's mother.

Matty thought the King of Kings deserved better than this simple bed, but he vowed to make it the softest, warmest, most comfortable cradle possible.

"We must work hard for this precious Babe," said Matty's mother, "even if the King's work is the hardest we ever do."

As the night progressed, the straw tickled Matty's nose and his tongue became parched, but there was no time for a sip of water from the chickens' trough. Matty's front legs trembled, weary from the strain of carrying the scratchy load, and his back legs ached from climbing up and down into the makeshift bed.

"Are we done yet?" asked Matty.

"Not yet," answered his mother. "It must be as soft as the down on the backs of Glenda's goslings."

On Matty labored. He squinted his eyes to stop a tear.

"Are we done yet?" asked Matty, tired as he had ever been.

"Not yet," said his mother. "Have strength, and imagine the perfect little Babe lying here safe in this soon-to-be soft manger."

Matty looked at the rising pile of straw. He could barely climb over it. His belly tingled and itched. He longed to be an ordinary baby mouse again.

"Are we done yet?" Matty asked, trying not to squeak. "It's so high."

"Yes, my child. Jump down and scurry over." Matty's mother nuzzled his nose.

"Good work, my son."

Finally, with the berth stuffed and padded, Matty laid his little brown head on his mother's round belly and dozed.

Just when his little front and back legs began to relax, he heard a noise.

"Is that the Babe coming, Mommy?"

"I don't know, Matty, but we'd better hide until we see who it is."

Scampering along the cold dirt floor, Matty tripped over a pebble and with a thud landed on his rump.

After Matty's mother lifted him and soothed his hurt pride, they perched behind a crack in the boards of Doris's stall and peeped through. Wide-eyed they peered until they saw their friend the Innkeeper come through the door.

Matty looked forward to the Innkeeper's visits because he always threw a little extra grain on the stable floor for their supper.

But tonight the Innkeeper brought only the cold wind in with him. It ruffled Mrs. Margaret's tail feathers. All the animals awakened and frowned at the unusually bitter gust of unwelcome wind. The cold blasts raised goosebumps on Matty's tender, pink skin. His mother pulled him closer. Following the Innkeeper was a man they had never seen before. Matty watched as the gentleman helped a lady slide off the back of a donkey like Doris.

"Where's the Babe, Mommy? I thought you said He would be here tonight," Matty whispered to his mother, his small teeth chattering as they struck together. He shivered in his mother's arms.

"He will come, Matty. The Babe will be here soon."

Matty continued to watch as the Innkeeper settled the couple in as best he could in the mountainside house of clay. He brought in fresh bundles of straw and mounded up a bed for the couple just like Matty had done for the Babe. Then the Innkeeper led the couple's donkey into the stall with Doris.

The Innkeeper soon left. Matty continued to watch the two strangers. Nothing happened; the two travelers simply lay on the soft hay beside each other sharing their warmth, and fell asleep.

Soon tired, Matty and the animals were asleep too. Matty cuddled close to his mother and slipped into a restless slumber. In his dream, he lugged more straw to a cradle that dangled high as the moon.

"Leap!" cried his dream mother. "Leap!"

All of a sudden an unfamiliar noise woke Matty from his nap. The wail of the Babe brought the darkened stable to life!

Matty could see all the animals stirring. The warm air coming from their nostrils formed a thin white cloud as it hovered in the cold of the night. Through the mist everyone gazed at the mother holding the tiny Babe.

How could such a small boy make so much noise?

His mother gently rocked Him back and forth in her arms. She wrapped the Child tightly in pieces of grain sacks the Innkeeper kept hanging on the walls.

Through the still and midnight dark, a faint orange glow shimmered all around the Babe, lighting up the entire stable.

"What is that light, Mommy? And why does the Wee One keep crying?"

"The glow is coming from the Light of the World, and the Babe's crying because He's cold, Matty."

Matty didn't understand all the strange things his mother was telling him tonight, but soon Matty's ears twitched as the lady sang softly to her newborn Son. Matty listened quietly.

"Hush, little Babe. Don't you cry, little precious Jesus from on high."

"Mommy, she called the baby Jesus. Is that His name? I thought you said He would be called the King of Kings!"

"Matty, the Boy will be known by many names, but He will be called Jesus by most."

"Baby Jesus," Matty whispered to himself. It had a nice ring to it.

The singing calmed the Child. Now the man took the Tiny One from his mother and laid Him in the rough trough softened with the fresh, clean straw Matty and his mother had layered in it with great effort.

"Was that my important job, Mommy—to make the Babe's bed?"

"Only part of it, Matty. The wind is blowing so cold through the stable tonight. It is very important the Babe be kept warm. My young son, will you crawl through the crack in the bottom of the trough and lie down at the Babe's feet? It is your choice, Matty, to accept or reject keeping this Little One warm tonight. It is your choice!"

"Why me, Mommy?"

"Look around, Matty. Even though you are the meekest and weariest one among us, God made you the perfect size for this chore."

"But Mommy, what about Doris? Molly? Tommy? Glenda? Randy? Lilly? Or Mrs. Margaret and the chicks?"

"You are the only one small enough to slip through the crack in the bottom of the trough."

"Precious the Moth is little!"

"But she can't keep the Babe warm as you can. You, my tiny stable mouse, have been called to this humble feat."

Again Matty didn't understand the words of his mother. Called? What did that mean?

"Many are called but few heed, Matty. Your innocent heart knows how to listen."

Matty heard all his mother said. His heart beat fast. He had never been in a strange nest away from his mother, but he knew someone must keep the Child warm. And he knew that someone had to be him.

Somehow he felt bigger.

He sniffed back tears. "I'll do it, Mommy. I'll keep the Babe warm."

Matty's mother hugged him tightly, holding him so closely he could barely breathe. He never wanted to let go of her but knew he had to. Matty shivered and lifted his eyes higher, then higher again toward the Babe.

He unwrapped himself from his mother and backed away toward the trough. On four silent paws he snuck his way to the Babe. From one stall to the next he made his way to the Little One, surrendering his will to the Savior of the World.

He knew to not let the man or lady see him. Why, they wouldn't want a lowly mouse to share their new Son's bed!

After a steep climb up to the trough's edge, Matty slipped and fell back down to the ground. But he didn't give up. With all his strength he climbed a second time, but when he was close enough to see the Babe's face, he froze. Matty had never before seen a real live baby. He spun around and teetered on the trough's edge. The little Babe whimpered, so Matty turned back to the Child. He knew that any minute he might start that loud crying again, so Matty hurried and slipped through the crack. There he nestled as closely as he could to the Babe. Feeling the roughness of the swaddling cloth, Matty let out a sigh.

He had done it! His heart pounded with joy.

Soon Matty was so tired he didn't even miss his mother. The heat of the Babe covered him, seeping into his little body all the way to the center of his heart.

The night was cold and long, but Matty and the Babe didn't mind, for they were together, safeguarded, secure in each other's warmth. Some might say Matty invented being quiet as a mouse that night!

No human ever saw the tiny mouse snuggled up beside the Babe. But the stable animals and Matty's mother did. They were witness to it all. They all shared in the miracle of that first Christmas Eve.

Matty, now a grown-up mouse, calls himself Matthew. He smiles as he remembers that night years ago. A warm, safe feeling embraces him when he recalls the night he lay curled up next to the Babe. He never forgets how he, a mere brown stable mouse, helped keep Baby Jesus warm on a cold evening long ago.

Sometimes while alone and quiet with his memories, Matty wonders: Did I save the Babe called Jesus on that night so long ago… or did He save me?

About the author

SARAH MARTIN BYRD is a graduate of the Institute of Children's Literature. She is a published novelist (*Guardian Spirit; The Color of My Heart*), newspaper columnist, blogger, and former advertising manager for a regional newspaper. Sarah loves sharing her life story with children of all ages. She speaks at schools, book clubs, libraries, and book festivals.

Sarah lives at the foothills of the Blue Ridge Mountains in North Carolina with her husband of 37 years. Her only daughter and grandchild live close by. When not creating new stories, she loves reading, camping, canoeing, fishing, exploring the world, taking daily walks, and spending time with her family.

About the illustrator

DEBBIE WALL, a member of the Pastel Society of Virginia, is a native of North Carolina and a graduate of the University of North Carolina at Chapel Hill. Her pastel landscapes have been exhibited at Virginia's General Assembly, the Cultural Arts Center at Glen Allen, the Center for Creative Arts at Shady Grove, and the Weinstein Jewish Community Center.

The author and illustrator were childhood friends who reconnected in midlife through their love of reading and of children's books. The illustrations of Manger Mouse were championed and critiqued by Debbie's adult children, Eryn and Tyler, by close friend and fellow artist, Valerie Olson, and by Susan D'Angelo Brown, an inspirational art teacher who first introduced soft pastels to Debbie over a decade ago. Debbie resides in Richmond, Virginia with her husband of 32 years and with their two cats, George Gray and Dixie Gray.

Acknowledgment

In my wildest dreams I never would have imagined an old school mate and I creating a children's picture book together. I want to thank my friend Debbie Wall for bringing *The Manger Mouse* to life with her beautifully detailed pastel illustrations.

Several years ago I wrote Matty's story for my granddaughter Emma for Christmas. This picture book is dedicated to her and to all children, young and old. I hope everyone experiences the powerful message this small brown mouse has to deliver.

As always, thanks to my editor and friend, Jo Martin. Who knows where tomorrow will lead us? I would also like to thank my publisher, Ambassador International, for believing in Matty's story.

I give God the credit for inspiring these words and for guiding me and Debbie through many obstacles while trying to finish this book.

May the God of all creation bless the outcome of these words. The seeds have been sown. Who will reap the harvest?

For more information about
Sarah Martin Byrd
&
THE MANGER MOUSE
please visit:

sbyrd@embarqmail.com
www.sarahmartinbyrd.com
www.Facebook.com/SarahMartinByrd
www.Twitter.com/SarahMartinByrd

For more information about
AMBASSADOR INTERNATIONAL
please visit:

www.ambassador-international.com
@AmbassadorIntl
www.facebook.com/AmbassadorIntl